# The Dinosaur Bone

by Elizabeth Dale and Stu McLellan

**W**

**FRANKLIN WATTS**

LONDON•SYDNEY

Rob liked dinosaurs.

He read dinosaur books.

He watched dinosaur films.

He even had dinosaur wallpaper.

But most of all, he wanted
to find a real dinosaur bone.

One summer, Rob went camping
with his mum, his dad and his sister, Jen.
They had great fun.
They built sand castles, dug ditches
and ate lots of ice cream.

Rob made a dinosaur in the sand.

The next day, Dad had an idea.

"Let's go and look for

dinosaur bones," he said.

"I hope we find some," said Rob.

"Me too!" said Jen.

"Come on then," said Dad.

"Get what you need

to go hunting for bones."

Rob got his fossil hammer,

dinosaur book and magnifying glass.

Jen got a bag to put the bones in,

and off they went.

They walked along the beach.

Mum and Dad looked up at the cliffs.

Rob and Jen looked down at the rocks.

They wanted to find a dinosaur bone.

Suddenly, Jen saw something.

"Look," she said. "A dinosaur bone!"

"Let me see," said Rob.

He peered through his magnifying glass.

"I think you are right!" he said.

Jen tapped at the bone with a hammer.

"Be careful!" said Rob. "Don't break it."

It took a long time to pull the bone out.
Rob took it to show Mum and Dad.

"It looks very old," said Mum.

"I think it is a dinosaur toe," said Rob, looking in his book.

"Yes!" said Jen.

The next day, they went to the library.
Rob looked at a big book.

"Look! The bone is from an Iguanodon,"
he said.

## Background Information

Corpus Christi College in Cambridge, and beneath it is an inscription in Latin that means 'What feeds me destroys me'.

### Are the characters in the Fanshawe Players (p.65) and the Henslowe Players (p. 139) real?

Some of the characters are real, yes:

- Edward Alleyn was a famous English actor who was born 1566 and died in 1626. He played the title roles in three of Marlowe's major plays: *Faustus*, *Tamburlaine*, and Barabas in *The Jew of Malta*.
- Thomas Kyd was a playwright who was born in 1558 and died in 1594. He wrote *The Spanish Tragedy* in the 1580s.
- Philip Henslowe was a theatrical impresario, who lived from 1550 to 1616. He produced a diary that is an interesting source of information about the theatrical world of the time. Henslowe had extensive business interests including starch-making, pawnbroking, money-lending, brothel-keeping, animal shows and bear-baiting, as well as running theatres. He established the Rose Theatre in Bankside, south London, and commissioned and produced plays by Marlowe, Ben Johnson and many other playwrights. There is no record of him working with Shakespeare.
- Although there were many theatrical companies in Elizabethan times, the 'Fanshawe Players' and the 'Henslowe Players' are fictitious acting groups, as are the characters of Harry Fanshawe, Trinculo, Monk and Christo. Trinculo is a character in Shakespeare's play *The Tempest*.

### Who was Sir Francis Walsingham? (p.86)

Sir Francis Walsingham was appointed Principal Secretary of State and Privy Councillor in 1573. He was born around 1532 and died in 1590. He developed the nation's first secret service, building up a network of more than one hundred secret agents across Europe. The operation penetrated Spanish military preparation and disrupted plots against the queen – including the Babington Plot, which resulted in the execution of Mary, Queen of Scots.

Dad and Mum looked on the computer.

"It says here that an Iguanodon
bone was found on the beach,"
said Mum.

"Let's check at the museum," said Jen.

The next morning, they rushed
to the museum.

A woman peered at the bone.

"Well," she said, "it is very old."
Then she smiled.
"It's a chicken bone from a picnic,
long ago," she said.

"Oh no," said Rob, "just a chicken bone!"

"You did well to find it," said the woman. "Better luck next time."

"Come on," said Jen, smiling at Rob,
"we have more bones to find."
Rob smiled back. Jen was right.
There were more bones to find.
Maybe next time it would be
a dinosaur bone!

# Story order

Look at these 5 pictures and captions.
Put the pictures in the right order
to retell the story.

**1**

Jen finds a bone amongst the rocks.

**2**

The bone is checked at the museum.

**3**

Dad has an idea to look for dinosaur bones.

**4**

Rob makes a dinosaur sandcastle.

**5**

The family go to the library.

# Independent Reading

This series is designed to provide an opportunity for your child to read on their own. These notes are written for you to help your child choose a book and to read it independently.

In school, your child's teacher will often be using reading books which have been banded to support the process of learning to read. Use the book band colour your child is reading in school to help you make a good choice. *The Dinosaur Bone* is a good choice for children reading at Turquoise Band in their classroom to read independently.

The aim of independent reading is to read this book with ease, so that your child enjoys the story and relates it to their own experiences.

## About the book

Rob loves dinosaurs! When his family go to a beach, Dad suggests a hunt for dinosauar bones. Rob and his sister Jen cannot wait to get started ... and they think they might just have found a real one!

## Before reading

Help your child to learn how to make good choices by asking:
"Why did you choose this book? Why do you think you will enjoy it?"
Look at the cover together and ask: "What do you think the story will be about?" Ask your child to think of what they already know about the story context. Then ask your child to read the title aloud. Ask:
"Where are the children going to look for a dinosaur bone?
What tools will help them?"
Remind your child that they can sound out the letters to make a word if they get stuck.
Decide together whether your child will read the story independently or read it aloud to you.

## During reading

Remind your child of what they know and what they can do independently. If reading aloud, support your child if they hesitate or ask for help by telling the word. If reading to themselves, remind your child that they can come and ask for your help if stuck.

## After reading

Support comprehension by asking your child to tell you about the story. Use the story order puzzle to encourage your child to retell the story in the right sequence, in their own words. The correct sequence can be found on the next page.

Help your child think about the messages in the book that go beyond the story and ask: "Why do you think they thought the bone was real?"

Give your child a chance to respond to the story: "Did you have a favourite part? Who do you think had the most fun?"

## Extending learning

Help your child understand the story structure by using the same sentence patterning and adding different elements. "Let's make up a new story about looking for crabs. Where could you go looking for them? What tools would you need? How would you know if one was real?"

In the classroom, your child's teacher may be teaching examples of descriptive language such as expressions about time. Locate the phrases relating to time in the story (such as 'one summer', 'the next morning' or 'the next day'). Ask your child to find as many as they can, and then think of some more examples.

Franklin Watts
First published in Great Britain in 2018
by The Watts Publishing Group

Copyright © The Watts Publishing Group 2018

Series Editors: Jackie Hamley and Melanie Palmer
Series Advisors: Dr Sue Bodman and Glen Franklin
Series Designer: Peter Scoulding

A CIP catalogue record for this book is
available from the British Library.

ISBN 978 1 4451 6215 7 (hbk)
ISBN 978 1 4451 6216 4 (pbk)
ISBN 978 1 4451 6217 1 (library ebook)

Printed in China

Franklin Watts
An imprint of
Hachette Children's Group
Part of The Watts Publishing Group
Carmelite House
50 Victoria Embankment
London EC4Y 0DZ

An Hachette UK Company
www.hachette.co.uk

www.reading-champion.co.uk

Answer to Story order: 4, 3, 1, 5, 2